ELF IN THE HOUSE

ELF IN THE HOUSE

Ammi-Joan Paquette

illustrated by Adam Record

CANDLEWICK PRESS

JINGLE-
JINGLE!

There's a girl in the house on this snowy Christmas Eve.

for Santa

Creeping down, step by step,
here she comes.
But—what's going on?
Santa's snacks are gone,
And the only thing that's left is . . .

CRUMBS!

So the girl goes first

on this snowy Christmas Eve,

Past the stockings and tree — quick!

Don't peek!

Then a quiet sound

Makes her whirl around,

And suddenly she hears . . .

a SQUEAK!

And the MOUSE goes second
    on this snowy Christmas Eve,
Marching on through the house with a wiggle.
Then a quick streak of red
Flashes by up ahead,
And suddenly they hear . . . .

a GIGGLE!

And the ELF goes third
    on this snowy Christmas Eve,
In a line dance of jingle-bell hop!
Festive friends in a row,
Down the hall they go,
Until suddenly they hear . . .

CLIP - CLOP!

And the REINDEER goes fourth
on this snowy Christmas Eve,
To a door topped with green mistletoe:
Season's joy gleaming bright
In a starburst of light,
And the *fifth* thing they hear? . . .

"Ho, Ho, HO!"

There's a party in the house
on this jolly Christmas Eve,
Sharing treats as the night slips away.

It's the best time of year,
Filled with holiday cheer,

And tomorrow will be CHRISTMAS DAY!

For Kate Fletcher,
with my thanks, awe, and admiration
A. J. P.

For my wife and three amazing kids
A. R.

First edition 2017

Library of Congress Catalog Card Number pending
ISBN 978-0-7636-8132-6

17 18 19 20 21 22 TLF 10 9 8 7 6 5 4 3 2 1

Printed in Dongguan, Guangdong, China

This book was typeset in Calisto MT and Sheree.
The illustrations were created digitally.

Candlewick Press
99 Dover Street
Somerville, Massachusetts 02144

visit us at www.candlewick.com